Biking for a Cause

By Rosa Nam, M.A.Ed.
Illustrated by Mirelle Ortega

Publishing Credits
Rachelle Cracchiolo, M.S.Ed., *Publisher*
Conni Medina, M.A.Ed., *Editor in Chief*
Nika Fabienke, Ed.D., *Content Director*
Véronique Bos, *Creative Director*
Shaun N. Bernadou, *Art Director*
Carol Huey-Gatewood, M.A.Ed., *Editor*
Valerie Morales, *Associate Editor*
Kevin Pham, *Graphic Designer*

Image Credits
Illustrated by Mirelle Ortega

5301 Oceanus Drive
Huntington Beach, CA 92649-1030
www.tcmpub.com
ISBN 978-1-6449-1326-0
© 2020 Teacher Created Materials, Inc.
Printed by: 926. Printed In: Malaysia. PO#: PO9231

Table of Contents

Chapter One: Wake-Up Call · · · · · · · 5

Chapter Two: Arrival · · · · · · · · 7

Chapter Three: Meeting the Team · · 11

Chapter Four: On Your Mark · · · · · 13

Chapter Five: The Medal · · · · · · · 17

Chapter Six: Not Giving Up · · · · · · 19

Chapter Seven: A Second Chance · · 23

Chapter Eight: Race Day · · · · · · · 27

About Us · · · · · · · · · · · · · · · 32

CHAPTER ONE

Wake-Up Call

"It's time to get up! You need to have breakfast before our big ride today." Jae ignored his mother and pulled the covers over his head.

Why am I doing this again? he thought. A few minutes later, just as he was falling back to sleep, someone pulled his blanket off. It was his little brother, John.

"Time to get up! Appa told me to come get you, so don't get mad!" John ran out of the room and took Jae's blanket with him, dragging it across the carpet and out the door.

Normally, Jae would have shouted and run after him, but instead he just sighed. He had signed up for the MS 150, an annual bike race that raises money for the National Multiple Sclerosis Society. It was a two-day, 150-mile race across Texas. Today was a practice race. Jae rolled out of bed and headed to the bathroom.

CHAPTER TWO

Arrival

The parking lot was already half full when Jae and his family arrived. Jae checked his phone. Judy, his best friend, was already there with his classmates and Mrs. Li. Mrs. Li was his sixth-grade language arts teacher and the bike club sponsor. She had invited Jae, Judy, and four other kids from

Thousand Hills Middle School to bike the MS 150.

Today's ride was six miles. The other practice races were going to get much longer—up to 50 miles! Jae was feeling anxious and glad that his mom would be riding with him for all the practice races and the main event. The two of them said goodbye to his dad and John and went to look for the team.

"Hey! Jae!" Judy waved her arms above the crowd. She was near the start line. Jae and his mom steered their bikes through the crowd to join her.

CHAPTER THREE

Meeting the Team

Mrs. Li was wearing a bright-yellow biking shirt and had a big smile on her face.

"Jae, it's great to see you! Are you ready?" asked Mrs. Li.

Jae nodded, unsure. Mrs. Li had special biking shoes with clips on the bottoms, which made her walk funny.

Her shirt had back pockets and she wore biking gloves. Jae only had on his sneakers and regular workout clothes.

Mrs. Li reassured Jae and introduced herself to Jae's mom. Then, they went to talk to the other adults on the team.

Judy pulled Jae into a side hug and introduced him to the other kids on the team. Jae only knew one of the kids, who was also in sixth grade. There was one seventh grader and two eighth graders. Before long, the announcer began talking near the starting line.

CHAPTER FOUR

On Your Mark

"Welcome, everyone, to the Jingle All the Way bike ride, especially those of you who are here training for the MS 150! For those of you who are returning, welcome back! For those of you who are new, welcome! We have plenty of signs and smooth country roads throughout today's ride. It's going to be a beautiful day. I'll be back in a few minutes, and we'll get this show on the road."

Jae looked around for his mom. A few minutes later, she returned. They reviewed the biking commands Mrs. Li had taught them: *starting, slowing, stopping, turning, debris, biker down, on your left, tracks,* and *bump.* There were others, but Mrs. Li said these were the ones you had to know to stay safe. When you heard a command, you were supposed to repeat it for others behind you.

The announcer came back and officially kicked off the race. Jae waited for the waves of bikers in front of him and then started pedaling. He hadn't known that the outskirts of Houston were so pretty. They began passing rolling green hills with white mansions that seemed to appear out of nowhere. Then, they biked a little more and saw barns and farmhouses nestled in fields of tall grass swaying in the wind.

Most of the trees were still green, but every so often, Jae spotted trees with bright-red or yellow leaves.

Jae was admiring the scenery and didn't hear the crowd in front of him calling out. When he finally heard the command, it was too late. *Bump!* Jae hit the bump and jerked the handle to the right, exactly what he was NOT supposed to do. He fell off his bike and rolled into the grass on the side of the road. The impact knocked the wind out of him. *Biker down!*

CHAPTER FIVE

The Medal

Jae had a large bruise on his leg. On the ride back in the support and gear van, Jae's mom held an ice pack on the bruise. Jae closed his eyes and tried not to think about the pain.

The next day, Jae laid on his bed and looked through Judy's news feed. He saw photos of the rest of the team smiling at the finish line from the day before. They each had medals shaped like reindeer hanging from their necks. Jae and his mom had received medals, too, even though they hadn't actually finished the race.

Jae looked at the medal hanging on his mirror. He had only hung it up because his mom wanted him to. *This is a pity medal*, thought Jae. He limped to the mirror, pulled the medal off, and dropped it into his top dresser drawer.

CHAPTER SIX

Not Giving Up

By Monday, Jae had made up his mind. He was done biking. He broke the news to Judy during homeroom and explained his reasons for quitting. He didn't actually like biking and didn't have time to train. He wanted to spend his extra time rock climbing instead and

always had lots of homework to do on the weekends.

Judy knew that Jae was scared of falling again. "You can't let fear hold you back," she told Jae. She reminded Jae of the time they were both scared of diving into the pool but then had learned to overcome that fear. Jae thought about how much fun they now had swimming and how he would have regretted not learning how to dive because of his fear.

"Maybe I'll try just one more time," said Jae, still unsure.

Judy jumped out of her seat to hug Jae and then sat right back down, remembering she was in class.

CHAPTER SEVEN

A Second Chance

Two weeks later, Jae was back at the starting line. The entire team was there for the second training race. Today, they would bike 12 miles across west Houston. Mrs. Li and Jae went over the biking commands. Jae was grateful that she didn't mention the accident. Instead, Mrs. Li patted Jae on the back and said, "You're going to do great!" Jae hoped so.

The announcer's voice boomed over the megaphone and started the race. Jae felt his heart pounding as he started pedaling forward. He gripped the handles extra hard as he crossed the starting line. His mother was next to him and gave him an encouraging look.

Judy called out from behind, "You can do it!" making Jae laugh.

The ride was mostly through the city. It was nice because people were outside in their yards waving to the riders as they passed by. However, one bad thing about biking through the city was the potholes.

Jae was able to bike around all the potholes until the tenth mile, when he came to a pothole so big that he had no choice but to bike right over it. Jae heard the warning up ahead and saw the wave of bikers come off their seats, dip into the pothole, and pop back up.

Jae's mother reminded him to lift

himself up. Jae pressed into his pedals and lifted off his seat. *You can do this.* Jae gripped the handles and dipped into the pothole. He pedaled twice and popped back out and onto the road.

Judy pulled up along Jae's right side. "Great job!"

Jae grinned and continued biking, more confident in his ability. He crossed the finish line with his entire team. At the end, even though this race didn't give out medals, he felt like a real winner.

CHAPTER EIGHT

Race Day

Soon, it was time for the MS 150. Even though Jae no longer felt like a beginner, he was still nervous. He stood in front of his bedroom mirror, wearing his full biking outfit. The biking shirt was like the one Mrs. Li had. It had a zipper down the front and

extra-large pockets in the back where Jae could put snacks and water.

This time, Jae was more prepared than he was on his first ride. He had long pants for the morning, a light jacket, and a small backpack for water. Jae took one last look at himself and walked out the door, ready for the weekend.

The first day was a blur. All Jae really remembered was the final rest stop before they finished in La Grange, Texas. There, the volunteers gave out free ice cream sandwiches. They were heavenly. Jae sat in the grass with his teammates and scarfed down his sandwich. As soon as they were done, they hopped back on their bikes and finished the full 75 miles.

In the evening, the team had a big spaghetti dinner. Everyone was happy to have biked halfway. That night, Jae fell asleep as soon as his head hit the pillow.

The next day was surprisingly easy. It was another 75 miles, but the energy of all the riders around him kept Jae going. As soon as they were within Austin city limits, Jae felt his heart beat faster. This time, it was because he was excited, not because he was scared.

Jae heard the audience cheering before he could even see them. Hundreds, maybe thousands, of people lined Capital Street. They held colorful signs and waved at the bikers as they zoomed toward the finish line. Some people even gave out treats like candy and donuts to the riders as they passed. Jae crossed the line between his mother and Judy and felt a wave of relief and pride.

On the way home, John asked Jae and his mother question after question: "Was it hard? Are you happy you didn't fall? Are you tired?" Eventually, John fell asleep, and Jae finally had time to think about the race. He pressed his forehead against the cold car window and smiled to himself. *I did it!*

Not only had he and his mom raised $400 for charity, but he had also overcome the biggest challenge of his life. He had biked over 150 miles in two days and faced his fear of falling. Now, only one question was left: what would he conquer next?

About Us

The Author
Rosa Nam used to teach high school students and now teaches future teachers. Her hobbies include rock climbing and hiking. She also biked the MS 150 with her friends and family, just like the main character in the story. The ice cream sandwiches were real and delicious.

The Illustrator
Mirelle Ortega is a Mexican illustrator, storyteller, and concept artist. She loves to read (and learn). She is a fan of science fiction, magic realism, classic film, and animation. She often draws inspiration from Latin American cultures and a wide range of subjects, constantly mixing the whimsical and the ordinary in colorful compositions that are both bold and vibrant.